Cruel Summer

About the "Author"

Johnathan Harker Heart is a lifelong resident of Vandalia Cou
Appalachia. His works are destined for the shelves of contempor
fiction and horror, but he claims there is truth, always, in the wri
word. When he isn't writing, Jack likes to visit bookstores and co
shops across Appalachia, and sometimes even find a mystery or t

Praise for Part 1

"The first installment of Cruel Summer is all the fun, campy
goodness of 80s slasher movies wrapped up in a fun, bloody nosta
package that feels like digging up a lost VHS."

@angelyoung13 Harley Quinnfluencer and collector, owner
@quinntessentialharley

"'Cruel Summer' is a wonderful little writen homage to one of
most fun genres: Summer Camp Slashers... What starts to set [it]
appart from its forbears is the writing, in the same way a Stepken
novel is set apart from their adaptations. You not only get the exter
happenings, but the internal thoughts and monologues which help
weave a rich tapestry over the entertainingly descriptive murders...
gels together into a story that whet my appetite and I really can't w
read the next installment."

Jimbo Valentine Artist and owner @amalgam_unlimited

Connect with the Q&L online:
QuillandLeaf.org
@QuillAndLeafLLC on threads and instagram

Part 1

Cruel Summer: Part 1
© 2026 Quill and Leaf Publishing

This is a work of fiction. Names, characters, place and incidents either are the product of the author's imagination or are used fictitiously, and any resemblance to actual persons, living or dead, event or locales is mostly coincidental and probably satiric

Published by
Quill and Leaf Publishing
Huntington, WV

ISBN: 979-8-218-87674-6

For Christy,
Fuck it.

Tommy

Tommy Cunningham was your run of the mill camp goer. Not too rich, not too poor, and dumb enough to do whatever the "cool kids" wanted him to. So, when he found out one of the younger campers had stolen some fireworks he immediately went and told Chet Fuller.

"How many did he grab?" Chet asked, immediately trying to formulate a plan on how he can get them from the kid. Original thinking and ideas weren't Chet's strong suit.

"I dunno. He's got a bag stashed somewhere."

"Any clue where?"

"I can try and find out."

"You do that. When you do, come find me. Those are mine. One way or another." Chet turned away from

Tommy to get away. He never really liked the kid, just kept him around in case he needed someone to take the fall for something. "Oh, and one more thing," Chet added as Frank Tooley and Terry Jones met up with him in their soccer kits, "don't tell anybody else. If you do, you'll find yourself locked in the outhouse with my dirty jockstrap as a gag while we party on the 14th. But, if I get my hands on those fireworks, you'll be front and center with us and probably get some pussy from one of the sluts in Cabin 8.

After Chet left, Tommy knew exactly where to go. The kid was constantly in the arts and crafts tent where they had set up some typewriters for some sort of summer pen pal program. Rumor was they were going to get a Macintosh the next year and they wanted to teach kids how to use the keyboard effectively.

Sure enough, as Tommy walked into the cabin he found the kid typing away. There were two other kids, nerds, also typing but neither were as focused as Michael J. Frederickson. His long hair straight like a girls to his shoulders where it started to flip like Farah Fawcett.

Chet even threatened to shave his head once and would have to, but when they went to do it the kid ran and hid somewhere with the adults and head counselors.

Instead, Chet and his friends had started a rumor that he had a twin sister who died in a boating accident and his parents were so upset that it wasn't him, they make him have long hair and dress like a girl sometimes.

Teenagers can be mean little assholes. And viciously cruel just to be seen as cool or popular. Chet was the worst of them. He didn't stop there. He had kept adding to the story every time some little kid came up to him nervously to ask him if it was true.

Soon enough half the kids at camp were telling stories about how "Michelle" was supposed to be in the girl's cabins. That some parents found out the girl was really a boy Fand thought they were going to try and fondle their daughters at night (which is probably happening consensually anyway), or he was just pretending so he could spy on them in the bathrooms.

Some really weird stories that just kind of dehumanized the kid and made him to be some abomination to be ridiculed and disgraced.

Tommy felt sorry for the kid, and thought that if he could get the kid to bring him the fireworks then he could become Chet's best friend, and maybe Chet would stop picking on the kid so much.

"Hey Michael," Tommy said as the kid finished his letter and placed the sealed envelope to be sent out in the camp pen pal program.

The kid looked at him, shook his head and started looking down as he tried to make his way out of the building.

"Hey, don't worry. Chet's not here. I just wanted to ask you something."

His head perked up a little bit and then focused back on the ground. "No. I don't have a vagina. And I never had a sister."

"No, that's not what I wanted to talk

about."

"Yeah?" He was hesitant. Waiting for the trick that he was sure was about to be played on him.

"Yeah. I want to talk about tomorrow."

"The Fourth of July?"

"Yeah."

"What about it?"

"Well, I heard some of the older counselors mention that some of the fireworks had gone missing."

Michael's face started to turn red and his eyes began darting around. "I... I... don't kn...know anything about that."

"Don't look so obvious. I already know you took them. I heard you talking to yourself the other day." Michael couldn't remember a time when he mentioned them, but sometimes when he's writing his letters he'll start speaking what he's typing. "Listen. I know that Chet can be a real asshole when he's showing off, but he's a really good guy. I know how you can make it so he never picks on you again."

"Yeah?"

"We're going to get together tomorrow at the story circle in the woods during the Camp show. Bring the fireworks and you're guaranteed to make Chet admit how cool you are."

"Yeah? Ok. I'll do it!" That was the first time Tommy had seen the kid smile.

July 4th

Tommy and Michael made their way into the woods. The dirt path had been cleaned up at the start of the season, but now cigarette butts and candy wrappers were littering the trail to the "the spooky spot."

All it really was was a small clearing where a fire pit had been built along with some cheap wooden benches. It was to the south of the adult cabin, which was more like a lake house, and easy to sneak off to during whole camp activities.

The adult counselors were typically too busy helping with the activities to notice a few missing kids.

"Now remember," Tommy whispered

to Michael as they neared the clearing. "Just be cool and I swear Chet will let you in."

Michael, clutching the canvas bag to his chest, looked up at Tommy and nodded. This was the moment he was waiting for. The moment his life would change from being bullied to being one of the coolest kids at camp.

Dusk had begun to settle in and the sun was starting to disappear behind the mountains and trees of Appalachia as the two boys approached the others. Chet Fuller was smoking a cigarette and drinking some bright blue drink from a brown paper bag. With him were Stacie Daniels, Terry Jones, and Frank Tooley.

"Tommy. My man. You actually pulled it off," Chet said, eyeing the bag the kid was holding.

"Yeah, I told you it would be easy."

"Awesome. Now, I have a huge favor. You do this for us and I swear, when we party on the 14th you're going to be the guy everyone wants to be."

"Sure, anything Chet."

"You need to go back to the

celebration and make sure no one notices we're gone."

"What?"

"You know. Make sure none of the counselors realize we're missing."

"But Chet..." He started to say.

"Don't be a retard. You do this and your dad gets us those kegs for Bastille Day then you don't have to worry about doing any snitch watch during the party and you can just chill with us the whole night.

"I guess. Can I at least see what the kid was able to bring?"

The whole time the conversation was going on Michael Frederikson stood still holding the bag. Nervously darting his eyes back and forth between the two. Until finally he said something.

"C...Can I come to the party?"

The group turned at the sudden interjection of the mousy voice.

Chet spoke up, "Show us what you got and we'll think about it."

The kid started to loosen his grip on the canvas bag and Chet snatched it from his hands, dumping the contents onto the ground.

Among the fireworks were the things all teenagers loved. Roman candles, firecrackers, and m80s. Two types of cherry bombs, original red and green ones kids dubbed sour apples. A few mortar packs (with no tube to fire them) and smaller artillery blocks. But what caught everyone's eyes the most was the bright orange flare gun sitting on top.

Chet immediately grabbed the flare gun, broke the barrel forward, saw that it was loaded, and put it behind his back like he was getting ready to rob a liquor store (which he had actually done before just to see what it was like).

"Woah, the little fag scored!" Frank said.

"What are we going to do first?" Terry asked.

"First, Tommy is going to go make sure we don't get caught." Chet reached down for one of the roman candles, lit the fuse and then pointed it at Tommy. "Aren't you?"

"Woah, watch where you point that thing." Tommy said.

The fuse was nearing the end of the

tube. "Better hurry."

The paper end burned away as the fuse disappeared. Tommy turned and started to run. He tripped as the first little fireball puttered next to him. Through the thicket of trees and the noise and commotion of the setup at the lake no one could even tell. Two more fireballs followed as he fled down the path and towards the camp.

Tommy made his way down to the lake area where the campers had gathered for the fireworks. Most of the adult counselors were busy corralling everyone to the makeshift amphitheater at the west edge of the lake. Others had the day off to go into town or spend the 4th so everyone seemed to be rather busy and didn't notice Tommy coming in late.

Everyone but Jeremy "No Fun" Runnels that is.

"Cunningham!" He barked from the risers donated by some church choir. "Where are you supposed to be?"

"I just ran to the wood line to pee."

"We have outhouses for a reason. Don't you know urine could attract a mountain lion looking for a fresh meal?"

Runnels was constantly trying to sound smarter than he was, but often got his facts mixed up.

"I thought that was bears and when girls were... you know... on the rag."

"It's both. Now find a seat. The show's about to start."

Tommy had just found a seat on the bleachers when the first bang went off. Tinny and high pitched. Chet had placed an m80 under a tuna can. The crowd turned their heads and quieted down slightly in anticipation of the annual monologue given by head counselor Watkins. More of the loud shotgun blasts of m80s echoed across the lake. This time the crowd turned towards the direction of the sound behind them.

That's when the light hit. A brilliant red flash lit up the camp from what seemed to be the campfire clearing. Then the scream. A whiny high pitched guttural animalistic sound of horror that only a child in the most intense pain could utter.

The crowd had stood at this point

and the echo of footsteps running down the aluminum started to drown out the terrible noise. Counselors and spectators were hastily moving trying to witness the carnage they knew was going to be at the end of that scream.

Tommy felt the goosebumps forming on his arms. The little hairs standing on their ends. Saliva started to gather under his tongue. His thyrohyoid muscle started to tense up and then he felt the push in his diaphragm. Tommy opened his mouth and unleashed a torrent of orange and pale liquid that cascaded onto the silver aluminum of the risers. The acrid and acidic taste of undigested oatmeal and citrus fruit covered his palette and he felt another push. This one, thick and slow. It dribbled out of his mouth as he leaned to miss soiling his clothes.

What had he done?

July 5th (technically)

Tommy couldn't sleep. He didn't personally see the kid's eye, but he heard stories throughout the rest of the

4th of July program. Other campers that had run up faster than the adults. Said it looked like something out of a horror movie about mutant zombies.

Nature's call had come across Tommy as he lay there with knots in his stomach unable to close his eyes unless he saw the horrific images his imagination could create. He had moved a trash can over to his bed but had only managed to dry heave when he felt the urge to spew. He got up, putting on only his flip flops. The outhouse was closer to the other cabins, and it was too chilly to walk all that way. A fog had crept into the campground giving it a ghostly white glaze.

Tommy ran between the cabins and pulled down the tight white underwear and counted down. 3... 2... 1. He felt a bit of relief as the stream started to flow.

Then the night went blank and his breath was taken. He felt the scratchy texture of the cloth on his face and the warmth of the piss as he stopped aiming and tried to remove the covering.

"Goddamnit, you got piss on me," He heard the voice of Chet Fuller say.

"He won't stop squirming." came the voice of terry or frank, Tommy couldn't tell with the commotion.

Tommy tried to scream but the cloth potato bag Chet and his friends had thrown over his head stifled him. A hand clapped onto his mouth and muffled the noise even further. They dragged him to the tree line, and felt his shoulder bruise as they threw him up against a tree. They tied his hands behind the tree and took off the potato sack.

"Listen here Tommy," Chet said, pushing his finger into the boy's sternum. "No one talks. We all walk. We were never in that clearing you got it."

"We should leave him tied to the tree," Frank Tooley said.

"Maybe we put an m80 down his undies," Terry Jones added.

"You saw what those things did to the tuna cans. Blew them right to hell," Chet said. "We're not going to do anything. Cause Tommy here is our friend. And friends don't rat on friends.

Wish you could have seen it Tommy. We told the little fag to run, just like you, but he had brought a flare gun. That thing was crazy. Like the biggest roman candle you could imagine."

Tommy felt the slack from the ropes on his wrist loosen up.

"Remember. No one talks. We all walk. They can't question us legally with our parents," Chet said, handing Tommy a flask. "Sorry to scare you. We just had to make sure you're really one of us."

July 5th (definitely)

"You're really one of us."

Those words were a mantra for Tommy.

He had made it. Nothing could stop him now.

"Cunningham!" The voice made Tommy stop in his tracks on the way to the mess hall for breakfast. It was Counselor Watkins. "Mr. Cunningham, if you would please come with me."

"I was just heading to breakfast."

"This won't take long."

Mr. Watkins led Tommy to his office where two sheriffs sat. A large camcorder had been set up in the corner and was focused on an empty seat.

"It's okay Tommy. We just need to confirm something with a quick interview."

"Sh...should I call my parents?" Tommy asked.

"That's... that shouldn't be necessary. You're not under arrest."

"But I'm not 18."

"That's okay. We're recording it," the younger sheriff said.

"Mr. Cunningham. We know you were in that clearing last night with some friends of yours." the older sheriff said.

"I..I.." Tommy started to say.

"A counselor, Runnels, saw you returning to the stands shortly before the incident with the boy occurred. Did you give the boy some fireworks Mr. Cunningham?"

"What? Did I give him the fireworks? No. He stole them."

"How do you know?"

"He told me."

"He told you he stole those fireworks?" the older sheriff asked.

"And the flare gun?" the younger added.

"Flare gun?" Tommy's stomach was turning with anxiety. "He had a flare gun?"

"Yes, as well as some fireworks, it appears an emergency flare was also taken." the older sheriff said. "But, he told you he took them? Did he tell you why?"

"He... he wanted to impress some campers."

"Do you know who?"

Tommy thought about the midnight rendezvous and he heard Chet's voice in his head, "No one talks, everyone walks."

"No, I didn't even know he was in the clearing."

"Do you know who else was in the clearing?"

No one talks.

"I don't know if anyone was there."

"Why did Mr. Runnels see you leaving the clearing?"

We ALL walk.

"He didn't."

"Are you saying that Counselor Runnels is lying?" Mr. Watkins asked.

"Mr. Watkins. Would you please leave the room. We do not want your input to potentially alter Mr. Cunningham's testimony."

Testimony? What do they know. Who have they talked to already? What do they know?

No one talks. We all walk.

And snitches, get stitches.

Tommy tightened up. Adrenaline rushed.

"He saw me coming back, but I wasn't in the clearing. I had to pee so I ran to the edge because no one would be able to see me."

"And while you were using the bathroom you didn't see or hear anything?"

"No, sir. It was getting dark and all I could hear were the campers getting ready in the stands. It was so loud from the echo and I was so excited to get back and get a good seat."

"Who did you sit with?"

"I just took an empty seat, I'm not sure who the other campers were beside me, but I could hear Chet Fuller and his friends talking about how cool a show it was going to be. That his dad had donated some really cool stuff that was going to make it a show not to miss."

"You say Chet Fuller was in the stands? You saw him?"

"I definitely heard him. He was sitting with Terry and Frank and Stacie and her friends."

"But did you see him, Tommy?"

Tommy could feel his heart racing. Lub dub. Lub dub. The sweat forming with every pulse. Lub dub. Lub dub. His heart was in his throat and under the floorboards and in the slow roll of the tape recorder.

"I think I saw him. I had to have. But I can't remember where. I know he was behind me. I just wasn't looking around. Isn't hearing him enough? Do you think he had something to do with this? With what happened to that boy?"

"Well it sounds like someone saw you in the wrong place at the wrong time."

"Runnels? He always thinks kids are doing terrible things. To him using the bathroom next to a tree is something to call the police for."

The officers laughed.

"We got the feeling he was kind of a tight ass. He's the one that said you were coming from the clearing."

"I only went behind a tree so people didn't see my... you know. I didn't see or hear anyone."

"Well, I think we've heard enough. Sorry to scare you kid."

"Is he gonna be okay? The kid?"

"Well, he lost an eye and is burned pretty bad, but that Nurse Bell is a badass. He just needs to be monitored and his wounds changed frequently. His mother is going to bring her some morphine from the hospital to help with the pain."

"Gee. That's awful."

"What's awful is we know he didn't pull that trigger. We just can't prove who. So if you know anything your not telling us, now is the time to speak up."

"I'm sorry. I don't know nothing. Wish I did."

Tommy realized he just used a double negative. Was he trying to get caught? But the officers didn't seem to catch it. Appalachians embrace the double negative in speech so often that it probably seemed right to them.

Watkins escorted Tommy out of the small conference room. They met Jeremy Runnels bringing Stacie Daniels. She had a smile on her face that Tommy saw often. It was a smile of guilt without shame. Tommy looked down and started running off toward his cabin. Tears welling up and dripping with each stride.

July 14th

Tommy got to Cabin 10 at 7 to help Chet set up the kegs that his dad delivered as part of a restocking of the small amphitheater. At the end of the year the campers usually put on a talent show to highlight the hard work and creativity they have learned at camp. One of the ways they funded this endeavor was through the sale of food and drinks. Don Cunningham, Tommy's Dad, worked at the distributor who supplied the camp with beer and soda.

Tommy had begged and begged his dad to give him a key so he could steal a soda every now and then. He obliged. He also happened to place an extra tap and two kegs unchained from the rest to help Tommy make some friends.

"Remember. Those aren't free. Charge a buck a beer and we'll make some money off those rich assholes Tommy."

Tommy and Chet had borrowed a wheelbarrow to help move the kegs. The two, with the help of Frank and Terry, lifted one in and Tommy pushed it to the cabin. Chet had this all planned out for a week.

"This is the night you become a legend Tommy," Chet said, trying to tap the keg. He managed to spray a good bit in his own face.

"Try not to drink it all before we get some," Frank chuckled.

"Yeah, Chet, leave some for the rest of us," Tommy added.

Chet shoved Tommy onto one the beds. "What'd you say?" He mounted him and put his knees on his shoulders. I should piss on your face for that." he started to unzip his pants.

"I'm sorry Chet, I didn't mean nothing." Tommy said, struggling to get his arms free.

Chet zipped his pants back up. "I'm just fucking with you Tommy, and the way I can drink, I might drink this whole thing by myself." Chet wasn't actually much of a drinker. For the most part he couldn't stand the taste of beer. He much preferred sugary, syrupy drinks. His parents would throw cocktail parties every other weekend and he would nab a bottle of rum and just add it to the fruit juice mocktails the bartenders would make him.

Chet got up and went back to the tap. It took him 10 more minutes, but he finally got it in. The boys poured their first cups of foam and Cabin 10 began getting ready for their party.

Cabin 10 was where the boys decided all of the "popular kids" would be. Cabin 9 was where everyone else would be. The kids would get to party in Cabin 8, and some of the other counselors who didn't want to party but still wanted to skirt their responsibilities and just listen to records were staying in cabin 7.

Eventually the foam turned to actual beer and the sun crept behind the trees.

"Party ground rules," Chet began. "Everyone pays. We're taking all the risk throwing this party while the senior counselors are off at their Bastille Day party in town. The only ones left tonight are Runnels, and the turds at cabins one through three. If they hear too much noise from us they'll rat us out for sure. Everyone stays inside. The less people roaming around, the less likely someone might check out what's going on. We need look outs. Two at a time. One person can run interference and the other runs back to warn us.

Everyone takes a shift, except you Tommy. Since you scored the kegs you get to hang out with us all night. Frank, you get first watch. We'll start when people start showing up. The best place would be at the edges of the shooting range clearing near cabin 6. It's got the best view of the road. If I know Runnels, he'll start a camp check at Midnight to make sure the empty cabins are empty. We don't want to fuck this up. Especially you Tommy. IF you want to keep being one of us."

Tommy, being nervous and wanting to really fit in, had managed to out drink the other boys who were sipping the warm brew and not chugging it. He could feel the buzz in his head. He was loose. Dancing around at the keg trying to get next to Chet. Trying to be the next Chet when Stacie and her friends walked in."

"I need a cup." She said, grabbing the red plastic solo cup from Chet. "If you're lucky, this cup won't be the only thing of yours I grab with my hands." She laughed and moved around behind Chet. Annabelle and Ellen flanked her on both sides as they stood behind the four boys pouring beers.

"Yeah, go right ahead. Your girls are V.I.P."

"Yeah, very important pussies." Tommy said, smacking Stacie on the ass.

The cup sloshed forward and spilled onto Chet's left leg.

"Watch what you're doing fuck head." Chet said, huffing with frustration. "You know what?" He huffed louder this time and puffed up his chest. "I think it's your turn to take watch, Tommy."

"What? Chet! I didn't mean to. Not my fault she's clumsy. I barely touched her."

"Well, did ya think the lady might not want to be touched. Or if she did. She'd let ya know first."

"It's Frank's turn. You said if my dad could get us the kegs I could hang out with you guys all night."

"That was before you decided to be a fuck head. Now get out there and keep watch. And ya know what, if you come back before 30 mins are up then you'll be out there all night. Even if we have to duct tape you to a tree."

Tommy didn't understand why Chet made him go out for the first watch. And to do it longer than everyone else would be. The joke he made was funny. Every one of them was probably thinking of the same joke. They made jokes about the girls all the time. Chet was probably trying to get with one of them.

It's not like he was actually going to. Everyone knew Chet wasn't actually any good with them, and that he was probably still a virgin despite all his talk. If he had had sex, Chet probably paid for it. Or his dad did. He always talked a big game, and the girls were just into his money. Guess that's what happen when your dad owns a dealership and your Aunt is a "big shot" politician.

Tommy stumbled his way to the archery range. The shooting line was under a small open structure to help keep the sun out of the archer's eyes so no accidents happened. About 20 students could fit comfortably on the line, but only 10 targets sat at the other end. The targets had been cut from a bale of hay donated by a local farm and tied with twine and spray painted then attached to large pieces of plywood. Not the most professional, but practical. A small mound of hay was behind them just in case. A pitchfork was protruding from its surface.

Tommy stayed in the shelter. He had a good view of the roads and would be able to see anyone coming from the northern and southern parts of the lake.

To the left was a cabinet that held all of the re-curve bows. The strings were kept in a box inside as well. The re-curve was a way to prevent kids from accidentally shooting one another as most kids couldn't bend the limbs to string them so there was no need to keep it locked.

On one of the shooting tables planted into the wood sat a small hatchet.

"Damn kids." He said to no one, and removed the hatchet. Then it hit him. Someone was probably using it to let off a little steam. He started to leave to take it back to the tools shed but then thought again. He couldn't let Chet down. But what had Chet ever done for him? "I bet Chet thinks he could hit a target from here."

The targets are a good twenty yards from the shooting line. Unbeknownst to Tommy, the fault line for axe throwing competitions was only about twenty feet.

He turned quickly and threw the hatchet. In his mind he felt just like James Bond walking onto screen and firing down the barrel of the gun.

The hatchet made it about 10 feet before it fell into the damp grass with a soft thud. Tommy heard the crunch of gravel and the snap of twigs off in the distance. He could see the north road from where he was, but no one on it. "Shit, someone's coming up the south," he said, and ran to the cover of the shelter. From the small lip at the shelter corner, he bent down and started to edge his head out.

No one.

"I'm hearing things."

Tommy started back to the spot he thought the hatchet landed and started looking around. He looked at his watch. Only fifteen minutes have gone by. He felt goosebumps forming on his for arm as the little hairs began to stand at attention. Fog was starting to criss-cross through the trees. Sweat formed at his brow. Tommy realized he had never been alone in the camp at night. Off in the distance he could hear cabins one two and three and the echo of the tennis balls from their Bastille Day tournament but it gave no comfort.

"Stupid Chet." Tommy finally said out loud, kicking at the ground in hopes to find the hatchet. "This is all his fault. He's the reason that kid got hurt. I had nothing to do with it. I only took him to him. I was supposed be able to party all night because of that. One of the guys. Frank and Terry didn't do nothing but watch." Tommy felt the hard wood of the hatchet's handle with his foot. He was about 45 feet from the target. He reached down, feeling the dew on the grass.

The hatchet handle was rough and worn from use, but the groove made it feel natural in Tommy's hand.

"I wonder what Chet would do if I brought this back. We could have hatchet throwing contests. Yeah. That's how I can get back into the top spot. I'll bring this back and we'll start a tournament. Bet I'm better than Chet."

Tommy moved closer to the targets, about 25 feet.

"Might as well practice for the rest of the time I'm out here."

He reached his arm back and let loose with all his might. The hatchet sailed end over end until it landed in the target with an echoing thump as it struck the ply wood backing. High and to the left. A wind started to blow through the shooting range, moving the fog in towards the camp. An old hinge squeaked loud enough behind him to catch his attention in the silence of the night.

The bow cabinet was open, and its door flapping. Tommy grabbed the hatchet and started to walk back to the shelter. He made it back to where he had thrown the first hatchet, turned and readied another throw, before bringing his arm back down.

Thinking about the events that had transpired over the past couple of weeks Tommy slowed his breathing. Envisioned the hatchet flying end over end and hitting the bright red center of the target. He started to wind up like he was about to pitch, bringing the hatchet down to gain some momentum on his back swing. He came down with his arm and let the handle loose. A splinter caught into his finger but he didn't wince. Instead, he watched as the tool sailed, slicing through the creeping fog in a small arc until the metal wedge landed just to the right of bullseye.

Tommy's eyes widened in disbelief and his jaw dropped.

"Holy shit!" he yelled. The words echoing through the still night. "Fuck you Chet!" he added throwing a finger out like he was really sticking it to him.

The waxy feel of the dacron bow string added to Tommy's expression of surprise and elation of his near perfect throw. He felt it tighten as he could no longer gather air. He fingered at the thin line and tried to turn to get a view of his assailant, but was getting weaker and weaker as blood refused to go too and from his brain. His oxygen levels dropped and his body slumped with no activity, the bowstring still tight around his neck. The assailant let the weight of his body strangle him further.

The assailant walked over to the target and pulled the hatchet free, sliding it into the leather cover on a tool belt. The metal tines of the pitchfork glistened in the moonlight as they wrenched it free.

They stood over Tommy's body and watched for the slow rise of lungs expanding. It never came. Laughter and cheers from the far cabins was barely audible in the still of the fog. Barely audible, but enough to draw attention...

Stacie and Chet

Stacie Daniels stood at the end of the pier. She was waiting for her best friends Ellen Summers and Annabelle Adkins. They were campers the year before, but this year they were all supposed to be counselors. Stacie was smart and passed the Life Guard exam the YMCA offered. Ellen and Annabelle however failed the CPR test. But that didn't stop their parents from going down to the office one day and accusing the lifeguard proctoring the exam (a black college student working part time in between classes) of being racist and failing them just because they were white and rich. So Sophie became a full fledged counselor and her two friends became counselor's in training. Which meant they weren't allowed to take campers out alone and typically had to do the more menial labor tasks.

So, they too got their certifications and all three had applied for positions as lifeguards at Camp Spearpoint. A couple thousand dollar donations from their parents, the camp had a new pier and the girls had their summer jobs.

Having just turned sixteen, the girls knew that the boys were starting to look at them and they knew they could use that to their advantage. On the second day, Ellen and Annabelle were supposed to be taking kids out on the lake for a canoe tutorial. More work than the lounging and sunning they thought they were going to be doing all summer. They didn't want to get their hair wet so they let a group of kids, including one with down syndrome, take out a canoe by themselves. Stacie convinced came by and then all three started sunbathing at the edge of the dock.

About ten yards out the canoe capsized. Most made it to shore safely, but the kid with downs didn't know how to swim, and of course they weren't wearing life preservers. The girls just sat up on their hands watching as he flailed about. One of the senior counselors was nearby luckily and jumped right in as the boy was going under. He swam him back to shore and started CPR.

The kid survived, but Stacie and her friends were no longer on lifeguard duty by themselves. Instead, head counselor Watkins put Jeremy "No Fun" Runnels in charge of the lifeguards and on duty with them for the rest of the summer.

Swimming became a less popular activity after that.

Stacie didn't care. She was still getting paid and she still wasn't going to do her job.

Then there was the day of the "incident," as the counselors started calling it.

July 4th

Every year the counselors took a raft out to the middle of the lake and did a big show. A few of the kids had managed to get their hands on some of the fireworks for the annual celebration. Everyone had been at the bonfire waiting for the show to begin when they heard the noise. First, the shotgun blast of the m80's echoing from under tuna cans they had secured from the aluminum bins. Reduce. Reuse. Recycle.

The group quieted down and turned towards the camp. Heads craned as the campers and counselors searched for the source of the noise.

Then came the light. A blinding red flash that lit up the entire camp came from the middle of the clearing they used for small campfires. Then they heard the pop. It was loud like the previous ones, but without the tinny echo. Then the scream. It was a little boy's scream. High pitched and obviously a scream of pain, not fright.

Mr. Watkins and the other senior counselors rushed towards the clearing. They found only one kid there. Rolling on the ground screaming in pain. He had his hands up wanting to put pressure on his face, but couldn't. His fingers curled in the agony as he held them close to the wound. The right side of his face had been blackened and burned. Blood cascaded and his eye hung by the optic nerve. The magnesium flare still burned nearby.

The camp nurse, Ms. Bell, arrived shortly after, pushing away the kids who were trying to get a good look at the carnage.

"Ho-lee shit," she said, drawing out the last syllable. If Nurse Bell thought it was bad, then it must have been. She was a volunteer nurse in Vietnam. "Son, I don't want to scare you," she said in her best bedside voice, "but you're in bad shape. I wish I could say this isn't going to hurt, but I think you know better."

She opened the waxed canvas first aid kit and found the pair of scissors. She then pulled out a small bottle of

rubbing alcohol and doused the blades.
With one quick motion she cut the eye
free from the socket, placing it in a 4x4
like it was phlegm she just coughed up.
She then grabbed her canteen and
soaked a bandage. She laid it gently on
his face.

The boy screamed in pain as the
open nerves that weren't burned
reacted to the cotton. She scooped him
up in her large arms and carried him
away from the clearing to the nurses
station, a wide room with four beds just
off the kitchen in the mess hall.

Everyone had followed Mr. Watkins
and Nurse Bell to the building, but only
them and the cook were let inside.

"What are you going to do Mr.
Watkins?" the cook asked.

"I mean, there is nothing we can do
for him right now. Nurse Bell will notify
the rangers and the hospital and we will
go from there. I will take the senior
counselors and we will finish our show."

"But aren't you curious how this
happened?!"

"It's obvious what happened. The
boy brought in some contraband

fireworks and blew himself up. Hell, I heard a kid last year that taped a few m80s together and blew a hole clear in the side of his brick house. Nurse Bell tell her that these things are closer to tools of war than we imagine."

"It is true. Fireworks contain real gunpowder in them. A kid can cut open a firecracker and put the black powder into a larger container and make their own dynamite essentially. We saw the Viet Cong supporters do the same thing."

"I just don't believe he acted alone."

"Well there is nothing we can do for him right now except make him as comfortable as possible. We shouldn't ruin the night for the other campers who obeyed the rules."

As the adults were having their argument, the campers had begun their game of telephone.

"I heard he swallowed a whole pack of firecrackers."

"I heard he had real dynamite!"

"I heard he's dead."

And so on they continued until finally Mr. Watkins came out.

"Everything is fine. One of our campers had an accident. We will still have fireworks if you would please calmly return to the beach," Mr. Watkins said.

Most of the children believed him and followed him to the beach. But not Stacie. Stacie knew what happened. She and Ellen and Annabelle all stayed back at the mess hall as the rest of the group made their way to the beach for 4th of July festivities.

"You know what happened. Don't you Soph?" Ellen said, her and Annabelle leaning in from both sides.

"Maybe," she said. She smiled one of those smiles where you know what that person just said was complete bullshit but they're not telling the truth for whatever reason.

"You were there weren't you!? Who was it?" Annabelle pried.

"You know that weird kid who is always talking to himself. Chet found out he stole some fireworks." Stacie said.

"So he did blow himself up?"

"Not exactly." That bullshit smile

came back to her face.

"C'mon. Tell us."

"Fine. It was Chet. That weirdo brought this bag filled with fireworks he stole to like get Chet to let him hang around or something. So, Chet said sure, and took the bag from him. At the bottom of the bag was a gun. Not like a real gun, but one for shooting fireworks or something."

"A flare?" Annabelle added.

"Yeah, whatever." Stacie didn't like being shown up, or having people act smarter than her. "One of those. It was loaded too.

So Chet grabbed it, put a few m80s in the barrel with it and then pointed it at the kid and told him to run."

"Did he?"

"No! The stupid little turd just stood there like Chet was joking. So, Chet pulled the trigger. Immediately there was this bright light and then the pop of the fireworks. Next thing we knew the kid was screaming. We all took off into the woods to sneak back onto the beach."

"Oh my god. What a turd. He should

have ran when Chet told him to." Ellen added.

"Right? Stupid little fag should have known..."

Stacie was cut off by the cook coming out of the mess hall.

"What are you girls doing here! Get back to the beach. NOW!"

"Woah. Don't need to shout." Ellen said. "My mom told me not to listen to anyone who shouts at me."

"Yeah, we were just heading that way. You on the rag or something?" Stacie added.

"Listen here you little fucks. I heard every goddamn word you just said. If you think you all are going to get away with this then you have another thing coming."

"I don't know what you're talking about. All that happened was some loser kid playing with fireworks and got hurt." Stacie said. That bullshit smile forming at the side of her lips.

The girls made their way back to the beach. Looking back and giggling at the cook as they did.

July 5th

The next day the rumors had started to weed out and the truth began to surface. A young camper, Michael J. Frederickson had gotten a hold of some of this year's fireworks as well as one of the camp's emergency flare guns. Others were at the scene but fled when the accident occurred. It became pretty obvious who was also involved as with most teenagers, they liked to talk.

Ellen Summers immediately told her camp boyfriend. Annabelle had complained to some of the campers that Stacie was leaving her out of things and told all of the girls in her cabin she was there. Chet Fuller couldn't help but tell Tommy Cunningham, who was their alibi at the camp celebration, what the m80s were actually like, and soon it was known that he, Terry Jones, Frank Tooley, Tommy Cunningham, and Stacie were the ones involved.

Of course, they all denied it to camp rumors when questioned by Mr. Watkins and the local police. Stacie used Annabelle and Ellen as alibis. Chet mentioned his aunt one time and the word "lawyers." That kept him out of the questioning. Terry and Frank just played dumb. Which wasn't hard.

July 14th

Stacie made her way by the head counselor's cabin to the secret smoking spot she and her friends had found. Mr. Watkins rarely searched the areas around his cabin for campers doing stuff they shouldn't be doing. Maybe he thought they wouldn't dare do anything so close to where he is, but sometimes the best place to hide is right under someone's nose. Plus, Mr. Watkins smoked himself and it hid the smell.

Walking by one of the open cabin windows she heard someone talking to Mr. Watkins rather harshly.

"You know that little shit Chet Fuller is responsible for this. Just because he has money doesn't get him off the hook."

"I'm sorry Ms. Frederickson, but the camp just doesn't have enough money to pursue a civil case against the boy and his family."

"It shouldn't matter. Everyone at this camp knows he did it. Him and those other little assholes. They go around gloating about their involvement. Doesn't that matter?"

"Not in the eyes of the law. They're teenagers. They have protections. Not just from their families, but because we can't actually prove they did anything."

"They've admitted their involvement to the other campers. I'm sure someone will speak up."

"The police have already tried to get someone to talk."

"Then you need to do something. Kick them out of the camp. Anything."

"Ms. Frederickson, if there was anything I could do I would have done it by now. My hands are tied."

Stacie heard the stomping of feet on the old wood floors coming towards the front of the cabin and made her way around back before they caught her snooping. After all, she was one of the kids they were talking about. She smiled and started to laugh but caught her mouth with her hands.

Ellen and Annabelle were already at their spot.

"You guys will never believe this." Stacie said, lighting up a Kool mild.

"What?"

"I just heard counselor Watkins talking to that kids mom. They're not going to do a damn thing. He said they CAN'T." She took a drag of the cigarette and passed it to Annabelle.

"You all just blow some kid up and get away with it? Rad. What other things do you think we can get away with?" Ellen said, taking the cigarette.

"I dunno, but I think we should have a party with the boys," Stacie said.

"Maybe you could even get laid, Ellen," added Annabelle.

Ellen cocked an eyebrow and dropped her smile. "Stop being a bitch Annabelle. Everyone knows you blow any boy that gives you the time of day. I'm waiting for someone that is worth giving it up to."

"Like, Chet?" Stacie said, closing her eyes and making kissing noises.

"Shut up. I only like him cause he's rich. He's got fish lips. Gross"

"And he's only 17 and going bald." Annabelle added.

The girls giggled and passed the cigarette around.

"Yeah, but he could afford a transplant or something," Stacie said. "Who knows. Maybe, I'll fuck him tonight if you only like him for his money. Seems like a good plan. You know, just in case my career as one of Charlie's Angels falls through." She struck a pose with her hands that was neither karate nor holding a gun, but some weird spot in between.

"Yuck. Is that show even still on?" Ellen said.

The girls put out the cigarette.

"Where are we going to throw this party?"

"Cabins 7, 8, and 10. They're the furthest from the counselors who would rat on us, and surrounded by counselors who won't. It's also Bastille Day. The employees that were working 4th of July have the night off and will head into town. We get all of the kids from the three party cabins into cabin 9 to let them have their own party for not ratting, and send someone to check on them. We'll also have groups of two take turns as lookouts at 4, 5, and 6 just in case every fifteen minutes."

"Wow, you thought this all out quickly," Ellen said.

"That's why I'm in TAG classes and you go to detention."

"Or because you and Chet already had it planned for a week now." Annabelle broke in.

I just came up with this idea on the spot." That fucking smile came back.

"Terry already told me about the party three days ago."

Stacie lost the bullshit smile and then put on a different one. "Oh my god, you slut! You fucked Terry."

The girls giggled and made their way back to their cabins.

That night the sun didn't go down until 8:53 P.M.

At 9:01 the girls walked out of Stacie's cabin wearing standard issue counselor khaki shorts and counselor embroidered neon polo shirts, pristine and bright against the twilight. There were three colors of counselor shirt, each representing a different seniority level. Annabelle and Ellen wore counselor-in-training yellow, or as commonly referred to by junior male counselors as CNT. Stacie wore junior counselor red, which was more of a hot pink.

The girls never took the required courses to be Senior Counselors, who got to wear pastel blue. Camp Staff wore Green, which included Mr. Watkins, Nurse Bell, Betsy Myers the cook, and the Williamson brothers whose main duties were to empty the trash cans and clean the visitors center and staff bathrooms.

Mr. Watkins and Nurse Bell were the only staff who had residence at the camp. Ms. Myers and the Williamson boys lived nearby on the lake and drove over. The Williamson's had Honda 250 dirt bikes they used to take the trails while Ms. Myers drove her '77 Jeep Cherokee through the access roads.

Stacie was not afraid of getting caught tonight and had decided that she was going to get with Chet Fuller just to piss off Ellen. It was true that he had wide lips that looked constantly greasy, hence the term fish lips, and his hair was starting to thin really bad. There was another thing Ellen was right about, he was rich. If Stacie got with Chet Fuller she could get just about anything she wanted this summer, a fair trade off for putting up with his greasy lips for a few minutes. Then she'd give him a blow job and she'd be done with him. She wasn't going to sleep with him.

That'd be gross, she thought. If he tried to pressure her she'd just say she was on her period. Boys his age were so grossed out by girls' cycles. Try having to put up with it every month. Boys can't even imagine what it's like to be a teenage girl and have your hormones raging. To be constantly worried about your looks while putting up with the looks of boys who have only heard stories of what to do with a girl from older cousins with little to no experience. From people who gave them a couple of porno mags in a duffle bag they found in the woods.

It was 9:15 when the girls had all of the kids safely in Cabin 9, and by 9:20 the counselors were strutting to Cabin 10. Cabin 10 was Chet's cabin and where the boys decided all of the "popular kids" would be in Cabin 10. Stacie walked in, eyed Chet from the doorway manning a keg he somehow smuggled in, and made her way.

"I need a cup." She said, grabbing the red plastic solo cup from Chet. "If you're lucky, this cup won't be the only thing of yours I grab with my hands." She laughed and moved around behind Chet. Annabelle and Ellen flanked her on both sides as they stood behind the four boys pouring beers.

"Yeah, go right ahead. Your girls are V.I.P."

"Yeah, very important pussies." Tommy said, smacking Stacie on the ass. The cup sloshed forward and spilled onto Chet's left leg.

"Watch what you're doing fuck head." Chet said, huffing with frustration. "You know what?" He huffed louder this time and puffed up his chest. "I think it's your turn to take watch,

Tommy."

"What? Chet! I didn't mean to. Not my fault she's clumsy. I barely touched her."

"Well, did ya think the lady might not want to be touched. Or if she did. She'd let ya know first."

"It's Frank's turn. You said if my dad could get us the kegs I could hang out with you guys all night."

"That was before you decided to be a fuck head. Now get out there and keep watch. And ya know what, if you come back before 30 minutes are up then you'll be out there all night. Even if we have to duct tape you to a tree."

Stacie considered herself sufficiently drunk enough to put her plan to seduce Chet Fuller into play around 10:15. Which meant she was drunk enough to put up with his fish lips and what would later be described as a "weird dick." All dicks are weird though. Chet's was especially weird though. Like a little mushroom tipped tube of lip smacker at the end of a forest of pubes.

"Hey Chet," She said, grabbing onto his shoulder and leaning into his ear to whisper, "Why don't we find somewhere we can be alone. I am so wet right now." She wasn't. Not in the slightest, but if there's one thing she's learned about teenage boys, it's that they have no idea what they're doing,and any talking like your a porn star was a way to get them eating out of the palm of your hand. "And, it's all because of you. You got a condom?"

"Yeah?" He said, and then it dawned on him what she just said. "Oh, hell yeah." He turned to the others and winked. "Yeah, there's a place we can go. Lucky cabin number 7."

Cabin 7 only had a few occupants. If cabin 10 was the popular cabin, then cabin 7 was for the nerds. Kids who would rather smoke some pot and listen to music, or play a board game. Kids who understood the hierarchy and played along because it was easier than the defiance they actually felt. If energy can not be created or destroyed, only transferred. They would never transfer energy to the douchebags in cabins 8 and 10.

Chet threw the cabin door open and

immediately fell into the table holding the record player. The needle skipped and the music stopped. "Everyone go party somewhere else."

"What the fuck Chet? Watch where you're going. That's a pristine copy of Rumors!" Adrienne Riddle said.

"That music sucks anyway." Stacie said, crossing her arms.

"Yeah, and this is now the make-out cabin. So unless you're making out you're somewhere else, and I doubt any of you all are going to be making out." Chet laughed at this, not knowing that two of the partygoers in cabin 7 had just left for the boat house

"Whatever Chet. We get it. Your dad owns a dealership and that makes you special."

"And don't you fucking forget it."

Adrienne removed the LP from the turntable and put it back in the sleeve. "Fuck this. I've got a joint we can smoke in the woods."

"Byeeeeee." Stacie said, waving to everyone as they left, until Adrienne was about to exit, and then she switched to a middle finger before slamming the door shut.

Stacie started looking at the available records in the milk crate before settling on The Human League. She and Chet then made their way to the couch and started doing what they had intended to do.

They spent 5 minutes with their tongues in each other's mouths before Chet started getting handsy. Two minutes rubbing her tits and he was starting to move his hand down to her thigh and between her legs. She kept moving it back to her breasts.

"Let's find a bed." Stacie said.

They went into the senior counselor's room, the only non-bunk bed in the cabin. Stacie took off her shorts and laid on the bed waiting for him to join her. Chet, being who he is, took off all his clothes. Chet wasn't overweight, but he wasn't fit. He had boobs. She couldn't help but chuckle. Between the tiny dick and breasts she just found it hysterical, and really unsexy.

His face flushed with embarrassment and the light seemed to catch the grease on his complexion and "fish lips."

An awkward silence started to grow between the two. Which is very out of character for Chet because he loved hearing himself talk.

"You can go down on me if you want." She finally said, forgetting the excuse she was going to use to get out of fucking him.

"Yeah?"

She doubted Chet knew what to do, but she couldn't help but think the fish lips had to be good for something.

Barely two minutes went by before Chet stood up, triumphantly. "You ready, baby?" He said, grabbing at his still flaccid dick.

Stacie was disappointed and it showed on her face. Her lips showed indifference, and then turned down in anger. "Ready for what?"

"My turn."

Stacie was not a virgin. She was pretty, smart, and always got what she wanted. Chet obviously still was, or he was just trying to overcompensate for some closeted feelings. Either way, she started to get the feeling that he wasn't even trying to show her a good time.

What was he expecting to happen?

"You expect me to go down on you after that? You're not even hard? And who could tell with that tiny little prick?"

Chet began to say something and then his eyes went from Stacie to the window.

"Well, you fucking fish lipped..." Stacie's sentence was cut short as the liquid hit her cheek, almost hitting her in the eye. Her mouth gaped in surprise. Another spray fell across her lips and she screamed.

Chet's throat had been pierced by the tines of a pitchfork. Arterial spray flew across the window behind Stacie as the body lurched upwards and then down in one swift motion. Driving the pitch fork into her exposed abdomen. The assailant removed the pitchfork from the two bodies. Stacie let out another high pitched wail that was silenced by the bloody tines. She felt the metal scrape between C1 and C2 vertebrae before she heard the tips pierce the cabin wall. She could no longer feel her lower body. The assailant stepped toward her, pushing the pitchfork deeper into the wall. Stacie's eyes widened in recognition before the darkness overcame her.

Annabelle

Annabelle Adkins secretly wished she was with her best friend Ellen. Why not? They were both rich, pretty, and in the prime of their lives. They would make the greatest power couple. Ellen had to know she had feelings for her? She had to know she was gay? All that talk of what they would do with boys when they came of age. Annabelle always went along but secretly, she knew it was Ellen she wanted to be with.

One time, Annabelle almost came out to Stacie and Ellen, but then Stacie started a rumor about some loser girl named Adrienne being a lesbian and trying to get everyone to ostracize her. Except the girl didn't care. She already sat by herself in the lunch room. She continued dressing in black sweaters and cardigans and carrying around a copy of Crime and Punishment.

Annabelle admired the girl after that, and wanted to apologize. When she saw her unloading for camp this year she thought, "This is my chance." But she never did. And she never would.

The only people who actually know what it is like to be a teenage girl are teenage girls and those that were once teenage girls. It is a labyrinth of social hierarchies, raging hormones, the watchful male gaze you start to notice from the boys your age, and even more terrifying, some adult men. Add being queer on top of that and its a whole mixed bag of fucked up.

Annabelle had always known she was gay, but in 8th grade she tried to date a boy. If you could even call it that. He took her to the movies and they snuck into Alien. He thought the horror movie would bring her closer to him and kept trying to get her to make out, but Annabelle was captivated by Sigourney Weaver. After the movie she let the boy finger her in the park. The entire time he did it she kept thinking of the climatic scene of Ripley in her plain white panties and t-shirt about to enter the sleep capsule. The smoothness of her legs, the tight fit of the clothes, the way her adrenaline was probably pumping after surviving such an ordeal only to have the thing attack one last time.

It was a perfect allegory for boys her age. Hell, the alien itself even looked like a penis. And the tiny mouth that grows from the alien's mouth? That had to be a metaphor for a hard on. Like the one she felt growing on the boy as he fumbled around not knowing what to do with her.

Then she started thinking about Ripley, again and started to direct the boy's hand where it needed to go.

"Ellen Ripley, last survivor of the Nostromo." she thought, getting closer and closer to orgasm. Ellen. The name popped out and she started thinking of Ellen Summers, her best friend. The image of Sigourney Weaver's face was replaced with that of her best friend.

This scared Annabelle. She stopped the boy who was trying his best to conceal his boner, or maybe trying to get her to do something with it. What did he expect her to do? The only reason she let him touch her was because it could be done discreetly and had already been aroused by the actress in the film.

"I'm sorry. I have to go."

"What? You don't like it?"

"No it's just that..." Annabelle tried to think what the best thing to say was. "I just keep thinking about the movie."

"Yeah, it was pretty gross when that thing popped out of that dude's chest. The way the blood just popped onto the t-shirt and he started choking."

Boys. They really do know how to kill a mood. She was planning on going home and finishing what he started, but now she had that scene stuck in her head instead. It reminded her of the childbirth video they were forced to watch in health class.

"Yeah, and probably not the type of thing you want to take a girl to if you're trying to get anywhere."

"Can I call you?"

"It's probably best you don't."

"Was I at least good?"

"Good at what?"

"What we just did? It was my first time, you know, touching a girl."

"Yeah it was great. I just wasn't in the right mood. Scary movies might make a girl get closer to you in the theater, but its not something to keep them close afterwards."

Annabelle wasn't quite sure if she believed that. I mean, just seeing that woman in her underwear sent shivers down her body. It awakened something. Something she knew was always there deep down.

It was her new favorite movie.

July 4th

The explosion came first. Almost like a gun shot. Then a few more loud cracks. Daylight emerged from the woods. The campers and counselor's were all distracted by the sudden brightness. What was a raucous celebration of the nations Independence had been silenced by the realization that this was not a planned portion of the evening's show.

Annabelle and Ellen stood up on the aluminum bleachers that had been donated by someone. Probably Chet's family. They were always trying to make a show like they cared about the community. Anything to offload a few more cheap foreign cars.

The counselors all looked at each other. Watkins had started up the trolling motor and was bringing the festival platform back to shore. They were waiting for direction. For someone to take charge. Runnels, seeing his opportunity to prove himself started to say something but was cut off by what sounded like the piercing wail of dying animal. Had some campers captured a raccoon or opossum and tortured it with contraband fireworks? All of the counselors took off toward the burning brightness. The stomp and shuffle of aluminum followed as crowds of children all took of with them.

"Stacie," the girls both whispered to each other. It was their responsibility to make sure that Stacie had an alibi if the boys did something stupid, like start a forest fire.

They started moving with the crowd. The counselor's were keeping the campers from going into the clearing which held the fire pit, and the screaming child. The girls walked through the crowd trying to get to a good position to see anything. The light had disappeared but there was still screaming. As they got closer, Stacie emerged from somewhere in the crowd and got beside the girls. The crowd shifted as Mr. Watkins held the kid in his arms and ran towards the mess hall, nurse bell shoving children out of the way. Senior counselors ran after them followed quickly by the crowd of campers. The girls lagged behind.

"What happened?" Stacie asked.

"We were going to ask you the same thing," Annabelle said.

"What are you talking about? I've

been with you the whole time," Stacie said. The sides of her lips started to creep towards her eyes. Annabelle knew that smile.

It was Stacie's signature smile that actually said, "I'm better than you and everything I'm going to say is utter bullshit. Now fuck off, or I will."

The girls caught up to the crowd. They heard some more screams as Nurse Bell attended to the boy. Annabelle figured they would cancel the fireworks show, but to her surprise, the counselors began taking everyone back to the stands. She, Stacie, and Ellen lingered by the mess hall instead.

"You know what happened. Don't you Soph?" Ellen said, leaning into their little triad.

"Maybe," she said. That smile crept back to her lips. Annabelle rolled her eyes, before feigning interest.

"You know that weird kid who is always talking to himself? Chet found out he stole some of the fireworks" Stacie said.

"So did he blow himself up?" Ellen asked.

"Not exactly." The smile came again. That fucking smile.

"C'mon. Tell us." Ellen whined.

"Fine. It was Chet. That weirdo brought this bag filled with fireworks to like get Chet to let him hang around or something. So, Chet said sure, and took the bag from him. At the bottom of the bag was a gun. Not like a real gun, but one for shooting fireworks for something."

"A flare gun." Annabelle said correcting her. Any opportunity she could, she would correct Stacie. Stacie was always trying to be smarter than everyone. And she typically was one of the smartest people in any room, but every now and then someone would correct her or offer an alternative, and you could tell it pissed her off.

"Yeah, whatever. One of those. It was loaded." Stacie added, visibly frustrated by her friend's addendum to her story. "Chet grabbed it, put a few m80s in the barrel and told the kid to run.

"Did he?" Ellen asked.

"The stupid little turd just stood

there like Chet was joking. So, Chet pulled the trigger. Immediately there was this bright light and then the pop of the fireworks. Next thing we knew the kid was screaming. We all took off into the woods and split up."

"Oh my god. What a turd! He should have ran when Chet told him to." Ellen said.

Ellen was really laying it on thick for Stacie. It was very unattractive. When they were alone, Ellen was critical of Stacie and her antics, but this... this was evil.

"Right? Stupid little fag should have known..." Stacie was cut off by the cook coming out of the mess hall.

"What are you girls doing here! Get back to the beach. NOW!"

"Woah. Don't need to shout." Ellen said. "My mom told me not to listen to anyone who shouts at me."

"Yeah, we were just heading that way. You on the rag or something?" Stacie added.

"Listen here you little fucks. I heard every goddamn word you just said. If you think you all are going to get away with this then you have another thing coming."

"I don't know what you're talking about. All that happened was some loser kid playing with fireworks and he got hurt." Stacie said. That bullshit smile forming at the side of her lips.

"Fine." Annabelle said, and started ushering the others. "Crazy bitch." They kept looking back and giggling as they found their way to the bleachers.

July 11

Annabelle lay on the bottom bunk of the bunk bed she shared with Ellen. They were both counselors in training, as identified by their yellow polo shirts they wore. Ellen had to take kids to the soccer pitch for the weekly tournament. Annabelle complained about some period cramps and got an excuse from Nurse Bell to miss the morning activities. Stacie was attending a meeting for the Bastille Day assignments.

Every year Camp Spearpoint used Bastille Day to give all of the senior

Counselors, who worked Fourth of July, a night off. Annabelle wasn't sure what was so special about Bastille Day, but from the context clues she figured it was the day Marie Antoinette gave everyone cake and a reason for celebration.

She grabbed the carton of Camel lights her older sister had sent in a care package along with a bottle of Malibu coconut rum. The rum was long gone, but Annabelle still had a few packs left in the carton. She took the soft pack and hit it ceremoniously on her palm to or three times. She wasn't sure why people did it, but it made her feel authentic. She tore open the foil top and popped a few up, grabbing one in her wine stained lips and lighting it with a cheap gas station lighter.

Annabelle practiced french inhaling. She thought it was sexy, and got about halfway done with the cigarette when there came a knock at the door. The cabin doors didn't have locks. For safety.

"Shit. Shit. Shit," she said to herself as she stubbed the butt and started spraying hairspray to try and cover the smell.

In walked Terry Jones.

"Goddamnit Terry," Annabelle said, slowing her breathing and calming. "I thought you were Runnels. That prick has walked in here so many times I think he's trying to get a look at the girls in their panties."

"Yeah, he's a chode. Ellen said you were skipping soccer so I thought I'd come do the same. Pass me a fag?"

"You're the only fag here Terry," she said, handing him a cigarette and the lighter."

"And what's that make you?" he asked through lighting.

"A dyke," she replied, reaching for the lighter and another smoke.

Terry and Annabelle had an arrangement. They both knew they were gay, or in Annabelle's case, maybe bi, and so they would keep each others secrets and be a light in a dark world of prejudice and misunderstanding. In doing so, they also pretended to be going steady while at camp. That way they can have fleeting moments where they get to be themselves.

"So, what did you come here for?"

"We're throwing a party in the far cabins on Bastille Day. With most of the senior counselors out for Bastille Day, Chet figured it'd be a perfect opportunity to steal one of the kegs from the amphitheater and go wild. He hopes it will help one of your friends to sleep with him."

"Ellen does have a crush on him." Just saying her name brought red fire to Annabelle's cheeks, but the reality of Ellen being a carpenter's dream, straight as a board and easy to nail, made the embers of passion turn to ire. "She could do better."

"What like you?"

"Like anyone but Chet Fuller. He's a one note momma's boy who has never had an original thought in his head. Hell, No-Fun Runnels is more attractive than Chet Fuller and that guy is a 26 year old camp counselor whose sole goal seems to be making everyone's life a living hell while they are here."

"Is this because you can't tan on the beach instead of doing life guard duty."

"One fucking retard almost drowns and suddenly, I'm not fit to be a life guard. I'm sure real life guards have done worse."

"Real life guards aren't 16 year olds at summer camp. They're like actual trained EMTs."

"Whatever. So, this party. What's the plan?"

"We're going to party in Chet's cabin. Cabin 10. Cabin 9 is going to house all of the kids, so they don't rat on us. This cabin is going to be overflow party cabin. Aka, the uncool kids. Cabin 7 will be for the weirdos that smoke pot and dress in black. No one wants them hanging around.

"Theres only like 5 of them. Why do they get a cabin to themselves?"

"Because if they don't they'll be just like standing in a corner drinking each other's blood or whatever."

"Oh my god that's so true. Fucking weirdos."

"So, since this party is going to pretty much be an excuse to try and get with chicks, and we're supposedly going together, what's the plan?"

"I don't know, but Stacie has been even more of a bitch recently. Like she owns everyone. It's fucking annoying."

"You said Ellen has a crush on Chet, right?"

"Yeah, why?"

"What if we convinced Stacie to sleep with Chet. But like, make her think it was her idea."

"Oh my god. It would piss Ellen off so much. So much that she might start hating the both of them."

"And push her right into the comforting arms of her actual best friend."

"Stacie would just deny anything actually happened. Even if they really do sleep together."

"Not if there's proof?"

"Proof?"

"You can use my polaroid."

"And what? Burst in on them in the throes of passionate love making?"

Terry laughed. The thought of Chet doing anything "passionately" aside from stroking his own ego, which he and Frank could hear from their bunk bed everynight, was a riot.

"No, but the senior counselor rooms have a window, and if you got close enough, you could take a picture from outside."

"Oh my god," she said, kissing Terry on the lips, which he quickly wiped away, "you're a genius Terry."

"Not a genius, just a vindictive bitch. Want to paint my toenails?"

The two smoked another cigarette as Annabelle painted Terry's nails with the turquoise nail polish he selected and started to form their plan. When she was done, she ruffled his hair, made a little lipstick mark on the side of his lip and sent him on his way so he could pretend to be something he's not for whatever reason he had. She had her reasons to. Hell. Half of Appalachia was queer they just didn't admit it or were too afraid to.

July 14

Annabelle and Ellen were in their secret smoking spot while the cabins all met for breakfast. It was a small area near Watkin's house. Mr. Watkins smoked, but didn't want the kids to know as there was a strict no-smoking policy for employees. Something about research ten years back saying second-hand smoke was dangerous or something. A few cities around the country were starting to make efforts on limiting smoking in buildings, but go anywhere out to eat and meat isn't the only thing being smoked in the restaurant.

Old men in dock worker toboggans chomping on cigars. Classy women with their Virginia Slims. Cigarettes were everywhere. So, it was no surprise the girls started stealing them first from parents, relatives and neighbors, and eventually working their way to petty larceny.

One time, they were really desperate, and Ellen had mentioned the record store her dad took her to every weekend had some Indian reservation smokes that just sit at the counter near the exit. Stacie immediately set up a plan. Ellen would go in first as the owner knew who she was and was always flirting with her about the latest sound equipment coming out Japan. Said they were working on some sort of system with lasers and discs that would make have to rebuy almost his entire inventory. She would play along, and get him to find something for her near the back of the store which held weird bands like Rush and Jethro Tull that her dad liked. Stacie and Annabelle would walk in, grab three packs and walk out. As soon as the bell rang and the guy saw the two girls, who's parents he didn't see on a regular basis, he stopped what he was doing and turned to greet them. He never took his eyes off of them. Stacie got nervous, chickened out and asked if Annabelle could use the phone. Annabelle dialed her mom's number, asked if she could stay the night with Stacie and Ellen and then the two left. The owner dipped his head and tried to catch a glimpse of them as they walked down the street. Ellen walked right by the counter, grabbed a pack, and walked out.

The girls loved smoking. It stifled their appetite. Gave them a little stimulant rush. And they felt and looked cool doing it. At least, that's what they thought.

"You guys will never believe this." Stacie said, lighting up a Kool mild as she popped out of the bushes.

"What?"

"I just heard counselor Watkins talking to that kid's mom. They're not going to do a damn thing. He said they CAN'T." She took a drag of the cigarette and passed it to Annabelle, who used it light one of her Camels.

"You all just blow some kid up and get away with it? Rad. What other things do you think we can get away with?" Ellen said, taking the cigarette.

"I dunno, but I think we should have a party with the boys," Stacie said.

"Maybe you could even get laid, Ellen," added Annabelle. "By me," she added in her head.

Ellen cocked an eyebrow and dropped her smile. "Stop being a bitch Annabelle. Everyone knows you blow any boy that gives you the time of day. I'm waiting for someone that is worth giving it up to."

"Like, Chet?" Stacie said, closing her

eyes and making kissing noises.

"Shut up. I only like him cause he's rich. He's got fish lips. Gross"

"And he's only 17 and going bald." Annabelle added.

The girls giggled and passed the cigarette around.

"Yeah, but he could afford a transplant or something," Stacie said. "Who knows. Maybe, I'll fuck him tonight if you only like him for his money. Seems like a good plan. You know, just in case my career as one of Charlie's Angels falls through." She struck a pose with her hands that was neither karate nor holding a gun, but some weird spot in between.

"Yuck. Is that show even still on?" Ellen said.

The girls put out the cigarettes.

"Where are we going to throw this party?" Ellen asked.

"Cabins 7, 8, and 10. They're the furthest from the counselors who would rat on us, and surrounded by counselors who won't. It's also Bastille Day. The senior counselors that were working 4th of July have the night off and will head into town. We get all of the kids from the three party cabins into cabin 9 to let them have their own party for not ratting, and send someone to check on them. We'll also have groups of two take turns as lookouts near cabins 4, 5, and 6 just in case every fifteen minutes. It'll just look like some kids took a walk."

"Wow, you thought this all out quickly," Ellen said.

"That's why I'm in TAG classes and you go to detention."

"Or because you and Chet already had it planned for a week now." Annabelle broke in.

I just came up with this idea on the spot." That fucking smile came back.

"Terry already told me about the party three days ago."

Stacie lost the bullshit smile and then put on a different one. "Oh my god, you slut! You fucked Terry."

The girls giggled and made their way back to their cabins.

The sun went down at 8:53 that night.

A pink cotton candy of a sunset. One

that landlocked Appalachians would still call a "sailor's delight." The girls proudly strut out of their cabin at 9:01 wearing their khaki shorts and colored polos.

They weren't supposed to wear the polos unless they were on duty, but Annabelle brought up the point that it would look like they were trying to maintain the order and not joining in on the rancor. Stacie brushed it off as a dumb idea, but when they had started picking outfits she brought it up. Said that the more SHE thought of it, the more it made sense.

She was always trying to take the credit for other people's ideas, and most of the time she got it.

The boys were already a little drunk. Of course they were. Especially Tommy Cunningham. He kept sloshing his cup and knocking into the other kdis. When they first walked in, he spilled his beer on Chet and then slapped Stacie's ass. Chet made him go do snitch watch by himself. About an hour later she had her hands all over Chet.

"I guess she did decide," Annabelle

thought. The funny thing was, Ellen had been nowhere near Chet all night. Probably because Stacie had kept herself between the two in conversations. Then Stacie did something that Annabelle had not expected. She leaned over to Chet's ear and whispered something. Chet's eyes lite up like an Addams family pinball machine going tilt. Whatever she said had done something internally to Chet and the two started towards the door.

Annabelle ran over to Terry who was with a group of the boys taking photos of some of the other girls. Girls who would eventually replace Stacie, Annabelle, and Ellen as the girls in charge. That's the thing people don't realize. There's always a power vacuum that needs to be filled in the hierarchy of high school cliques and groups. It just so happens that it's typically the ones with money and the connections to get away with their bullshit that are often at the top. Which makes those at the bottom resort to more and more drastic measures to make that power gap just a little bit smaller. Which often leads to worse and worse consequences. Especially for the people of color who have had to deal with systemic racism all their lives.

"Terry. It's time. I need the polaroid."

"One second," He said. One of the boys he was with got down behind one of the other boys and pulled both legs of the shorts down in one swift motion. For a brief second the boy was fully exposed and in that brief moment the flash went off on the polaroid and an undeveloped photo popped out the front. Terry took the photo out and started shaking it like a southern belle shaking a fan in a hot Georgia summer before he put it away. "I'll save that for later," he said before handing the camera to Annabelle.

She ran to to the back of the cabin and out the door. She could see the couple making their way north on the path. Staying behind the cabins Annabelle followed them. They didn't take the turn to go into the heart of the camp, but instead made their way further north.

Cabins 8 and 9 were loud and Annabelle could see the shadows of kids having a good time. Not worried about anything other than having fun. Annabelle crept around as close to the building as possible, careful not to let her body cast shadows in dimness beind the cabins. Each cabin had a small light by the backdoor but it was caged because kids kept breaking the bulbs or unscrewing them to hide their devious camp schemes. Schemes like the one Annabelle was about to complete.

Chet and Stacie made their way to the front door of cabin 7. Annabelle slipped in behind the rhododendrons and carefully lift her head above the windowsill. Chet and Stacie seemed to be arguing with Adrienne Riddle. The music had stopped when the two went through the front door but it still was hard for Annabelle to figure out what they were saying. The cabin 7 kids started to head out the front door as Stacie started searching through the record collection. Chet was sitting on the couch grabbing at his crotch when Ananbelle started to hear the muffled sounds of The Human League playing from the speakers.

"If they're going to do anything they're going to head to the counselor's room." Annabelle thought. "They know the outside doors don't lock and wouldn't want anyone to bust in without their knowing it." She waited patiently beneath the rhodedendron as the two began kissing on the couch. Annabelle started to laugh at what she was seeing.

Chet was so bad at kissing. He kept opening his mouth way too much like he was one of those fish her dad had that cleaned the sides of the fish tank as it moved around. He was everywhere. His fish lips attacking at her tongue like it was a double scoop pineapple grape from Austin's in a homemade waffle cone. And his hands. Its like he didn't know what to do. At one point Annabelle thought he was petting her head like she did Mr. Wumpkins her orange tabby. She could tell Stacie was getting bored because she started to redirect him, and finally she stopped him all together.

"I wouldn't be surprised if she just started yelling at him." Annabelle thought, chuckling lightly at the idea of Chet getting humiliated by Stacie. To her surprise, Stacie instead got up, and pulled Chet's hand to follow her. "SHE'S TAKING HIM!" Annabelle shouted in her head. She crashed out the rhodedendrons, scratching her ankles and her cheek on a couple of sharp branches.

The counselor's room was at the rear and had a single window at the back that looked onto the forest behind them. Annabelle watched as Stacie flicked the light on. The room illuminated in the window. Annabelle could see right in. Stacie seemed to be getting an idea of what she was going to do and turned to pull down her shorts. When she turned, Annabelle caught a glimpse of Chet in the doorway behind her. He was already naked!

"Oh my god, who does that?" Annabelle said out loud. Almost too loud. It carried softly in the night air. She could no longer See Stacie from her position. The window was just a little too high, but she could still she Chet. Chet's head went down from view.

"Those fish lips must be good for that," Annabelle thought, and for a moment she imagined it. But then the thought of who it actually was came to the foe front of her imagination. The mineral taste of alcohol and vomit crept up her throat and she gagged.

Chet must have heard the noise because he started looking hard at the window. Like he was trying to get a better glimpse of what he saw. She snapped a picture real quick. The flash lit up the area outside of the window with its glamour. The buzz and whir of the polaroid as it spit out the photo made Annabelle jump.

"Shit, shit, shit." she said and looked back into the window.

Chet Fuller was being hoisted into the air, four black spots of dripping blood running down his body as it fell down in a swift motion. A high pitched guttural scream erupting from Stacie. Annabelle saw the assailant pull back a pitchfork and bring it forward with all their might and Stacie's scream ended.

"What do I do. What do I do?" Annabelle asked and before she could think, she brought the polaroid up on more time and snapped another picture. Whoever had just attacked Stacie and Chet must have seen the flash because Annabelle saw them turn and rush out the door. "They're coming to get me. What do I do?" Annabelle was trying desperately to make conscious decisions. Several different thoughts ran through her head. "SCREAM. YELL. RUN. MOVE." she heard her mind trying to convince her to just act on any of them. She sat there. Frozen. The camera whirring as the photo popped out. She grabbed it and placed it in her pocket with the other photo.

The back door slammed closed and brought Annabelle back to her senses. The assailant was burling towards her, nearly 10 ft away or less. Annabelle pulled the camera up once again.

"Say cheese!" she said, and snapped another photo, this time aiming the flash right in her attacker's eyes. Then she did the smartest thing she had ever done. She took off running. The camera whirred and buzzed and pushed out the photo. She dropped the camera pulling the photo and tried to shake it to make it develop faster, but her concentration had been focused on the singular act of getting the fuck out of there.

She didn't even realize she was heading west into the woods until she almost collided with a tree that seemed to come out of no where.

Annabelle was surprised by how well her body took over in this instance. She remembered briefly her high school biology teacher tell them about the nervous system and the fight or flight response. How some mothers in the adrenaline of an extreme situation involving their children are capable of inhuman feats of strength. Like moving entire cars by themselves to free a trapped baby.

Almost as soon as she started to realize these feelings and think about what her body was doing it caught up to her. Fire erupted in her lungs with every breath she pushed out. Her side tightened into a stitch like the worst of period cramps. The kind her mom complained about at 42 and found out she had started menopause early. That was right around the time her dad started flirting with his assistant at work.

Annabelle started thinking about how she might never get to see her dad again. And how she'd tell that bitch Brenda she would never be her mother. She kept running zigzagging through the trees to make it harder to follow until finally Annabelle could no longer hear the footfalls behind her.

"That's right. Give up you stupid mother fucker." She whispered, and pulled herself behind the next tree big enough to hide her size 12 body.

"Breathe," she heard her mind telling her body. As she took deep gasps, trying to gather as much air as she could in case she had to make another run. "How far did I go, she started to wonder." When they had to do the mile in gym class it had taken her about 13 minutes to complete. Had she been running for that long?" She got conscious of how loud she was breathing and tried to do slow shallow breaths. She started to peak out from behind her tree when she heard the slow footfall of heavy boots shuffling through the leaves and brush. "Must figure out where I am," she thought.

On the first week, Watkins had taken all of the counselor in training and counselors into the wood for a lesson on the trail markers. The other thing he did was show how one can end up walking around in circles despite thinking you're going in a straight line without markers. Had she circled back on herself? Was the person who attacked Stacie and Chet still behind her, or were they in front?

They had to be behind if they were still there. Perhaps they saw her get too far ahead and decided it wasn't worth their time. Maybe they went back to make sure they completed the job. Annabelle turned around as if she was hugging the tree like when they made fun of the vegan kid Carly, and peeked from the safety of the trunk. It was dark and her eyes had finally adjusted, but she could only see the shadows and hear the sounds of leaves crunching and twigs cracking. Every pop made her startle and turn towards the sound, but she couldn't make out her assailant.

 She definitely understood WHY someone would want to kill Chet and Stacie, but now, Annabelle was a witness. A loose end. "Plus, you got a picture of them," she said to herself. Her head kicked up at the recognition of what she just thought. "I got a picture of the killer!" The words came out loud with excitement. Still gripping the side of the tree with her left hand as she reached into her pocket with her right. Looking down, she saw the photo of Chet standing there with his tiny dick staring at the window. The assailant a shadow behind him. She carefully dropped the photo as she held onto the other two.

She pulled the two photos up to her eyes to get as good a look as she could, but got distracted by the resonant "Thunk" of metal into wood. Warmth cascaded down the front of her palm. She pulled back her left hand in terror. A hatchet with a well worn handle and bright blade had been sank into the tree. Her palm had shattered and split at the ring finger. It flopped, held on by the ligaments and muscle of her wrist. And then her head rushed forwards as her face slammed into the tree. Her front teeth pushing backward towards the roof of her mouth, ruining the two years of braces she suffered through. Annabelle was still conscious, nerves firing all over body as she felt her body and head turning towards her assailant. Through the pain the rough hands gripped her head and she felt the soft tearing and then pop as the thumbs pushed deep into her occular cavity and then swirl.

Annabelle slid down the tree trunk, her back scraping against the rough bark. The scream she let out was a scream of recognition. Not at her assailant, whom she would never see, but at the thought...

But there was no thought. The attacker had pulled the hatchet free and with one swift motion, planted it just as deep in Annabelle's skull. Annabelle's killer picked up the two photos, looked at the first and then threw it on the ground. The window had caught the flash and reflected it back onto the film, overexposing it with light and creating nothing but a bright white image. The other. The other they crumpled up, took a lighter from their pocket, and lit it, dropping it onto Annabelle's body. The synthetic fibers of her shirt, soaked in the alcohol and oils of her perfume, catching and melting onto the lifeless skin. A beam of light flickered nearby crossing several trees, but never landing on Annabelle or her attacker. The attacker put a dirty boot on Annabelle's shoulder and held her against the tree for leverage, pulling the hatchet free from its cranial sheath and moving in the direction from which the light had shone.

**Continued in
Cruel Summer: Part 2**

Coming Later from Quill and Leaf

More in the Vandalia County Video
Nasties Series

ruel Summer: Part 2 (2027)
ruel Summer: The Final POV (TBD)
other (TBD)
reamweaver (TBD)

Blank Case-ettes

Vandalia County Almanac

Please enjoy a sneak preview of the
Vandalia County Almanac:
Stories for and from Appalachia

Featuring Authors

Catherine Herlihy
Christopher Tucker

If you are interested in helping rewrite the
narrative for Appalachia, please email
Submissions@quillandleaf.org or visit
quillandleaf.org

Fasnacht

by Catherine Herlihy

Virginia stood in her room brushing her dark hair and gazing out the window at the eiderdown of snow that had rested into the hollows overnight. She wound thick strands around her fingers and pinned each curl in place. The potholes on the main dirt road had been crystallized into a sheen of white, and the clashing colors on her neighbor's barn had been erased. The snow made those things just a memory. Soon the sunny crocuses would start to poke their way through from the underworld where they had been hiding in the black wetness of eternity, the place where life decomposes and is reborn. Tonight, Virginia wanted to dance in the darkness of winter before the earth began to thaw as the people of Helvetia burned Old Man Winter on his funeral pyre.

Outside the people of the town were preparing for the evening's Fasnacht festivities. Boys chased each other wearing paper-mâché masks, each bird beak and antlered beast more elaborate than the last. The caretaker swept the dust out the golden doors of the Star Band Hall to get ready for the evening's dancing. Virginia watched the preacher with his head bent making his way down the middle of the street toward the church. He glanced up at her house as he went by. She tapped on the window and waved. His face strained into a weak smile, and he turned from her to continue on his way.

Across the street Hattie and Nell stood on the front porch in their quilted bathrobes, steamy mugs of milky sweet tea in their hands. Their heads bent toward each other, and Virginia watched

their lips strike like matches. They made furtive swivels and peeks in her direction, and Virginia felt a sickening tug in her abdomen. She knew what they thought of her, but she scattered the thoughts from the edges of her mind. This was her day.
She could hear Matthias on the other end of the house busying himself. He was probably having his morning coffee and reading the newspaper before getting into his suit. She couldn't wait for him to see her in her dress.

"Matthias? Are you getting ready yet?" she called to the other end of the house.

"Soon, my love. Soon." He called back, his deep voice carrying down the hallway. Her heart quickened in delight. She had never felt more sure of anything.
He'd asked for her hand after the Epiphany feast. Their bellies were bursting with meat pies and Basel cookies, and they were warm from the gluhwein. Matthias hid the small gold ring in his trouser pocket and secretly doused it with holy water. Their heads

ached from the thick incense, and their clothes smelled of myrrh. He wore a crooked foil crown for the Magi, and they'd snuck out into the forest protected by the Holy Ghost.

Each branch of the cottonwood tree at the edge of the town had been encased in ice, dangling mirrors casting light from dying stars. It was under this frozen chandelier that he'd kissed her, their lips brushing softly at first. Everything had rippled to life inside her. He took off her woolen glove, and she'd protested because of the cold. He'd held her blue fingers between his and breathed warmth on them before slipping the small ring on her finger. His lashes and copper beard caught snow crystals, sparkling like allotropes.

She had felt clear-eyed and quick like one of the other beasts in the woods on this frosty night. Of course they would spend their lives together. She had taken his hand and leaped across a snowdrift, oblivious to the cold with apple cheeks and cherry noses and guided by the ghosts that came before them.

From down the hall, his nimble fingers began to pluck at his mandolin, and her slippered feet shuffled lightly across the wooden planks of her floor. She knew those hands, those dexterous fingers that whittled wood and plaited her thick hair across his chest while their cold toes found each other at the bottom of the bed and tried furiously to warm themselves in the winter night. The dress hung from her mirror in the corner of the room. Her grandmother had made the dress, her bent, arthritic fingers braiding lacey webs of thread around wooden bobbins and satin pins, expert as an orb weaver. She had marveled at this dress since she was a child, and now it was like having the other women there with her eagerly awaiting the moment she would walk down the aisle as each of them had on their wedding day. She ran her fingers along the fine lace of the sleeves like brittle bone and held each of them in her hands in greeting.

Virginia let her lover's flannel robe slip from her shoulders as she took the dress from its hanger. With steady hands, she held the skirt open, careful not to rip the decaying silk, and stepped inside. She thought of the worms that worked to make their silver silken cocoons that were to become her gown. It took her some time to work the buttons of the bodice, but when she was finished she was enshrined in the dusty white dress. It no longer mattered if the past were the future or the future were the past.

The strand of pearls fastened around her neck felt slippery and smooth as teeth across her collar bone. She fiddled with the gold band on her left hand. It was time for the finishing touches. The mirror of her dressing table was cracked and marbled with age. Virginia cocked the blade with the little hook on her spring lancet, and careful to hold her hand angled away from her dress, she pressed the button on the side. A red rivulet of blood bubbled down her hand, and she pressed the leaky finger into her tin of beeswax. She massaged the pigment onto her cheeks, giving them a pinch and dabbed her lips. Inspecting her face close to the warped mirror, she imagined the wrinkles around her eyes and at the corners of her mouth growing deeper over the years, her face becoming more her own. She pressed her lips together roughly. The comb of her veil dug into the back of her scalp, and she gave it a little wiggle to make it settle into place. Virginia tiptoed over to Matthias's bureau and slid out the bottom drawer. Sitting on her knees, she buried her nose in his undershirts. Though they had been laundered, they smelled of basswood and sweet sweat from his workshop. The coin collection was hidden beneath his socks. She chose two of the prettiest and placed one in each boot. Her stockinged feet slid into the leather, stiff from being dried next to the fire, and her toes found the silver coins. They felt smooth and metallic through her stockings.

She opened her front door. She couldn't hear Matthias at the back of the house anymore and thought he must be waiting for her at the church altar. In her excitement, she didn't remember to close the door behind her as she made her way across the porch, down the front steps and out into the snow. Cold air blustered through the rooms of the house, stirring the lace curtains, ruffling the pages of Matthias's newspaper which still sat beside a cup of cold coffee, and blowing a kiss to the dying embers of the fire, extinguishing them completely. Ahead of her on the road a hundred candles burned in the Fasnacht procession toward the town square. Bear, raven, and human chimeras walked in serious succession toward the sacrifice. Daemons danced around the edges, and witches and jesters lilted lightly behind. They were carrying the effigy of Old Man Winter on their shoulders, ready to play out the murder ballad around the warmth of his funeral pyre with prayers for the spring to hurry fast.

As she pulled open the heavy oak doors at the back of the church, there was a collective heaving breath from the pews. The church was nearly full, a sea of serious black suits and dresses on each side of the aisle.

She bent to take off each of her snowy boots and set them to the side. The bottom of her dress was wet and withered. Exhuming each warm coin, she held the silver in one hand and a bouquet of aubergine calla lilies in the other in front of her heart. Virginia smiled demurely at the guests from beneath her veil before she saw her love at the other end of the aisle. Her lips broadened, and her eyes gleamed in delight. Blinking fast to keep the tears from coming, she swished slowly in stockinged feet down the aisle.

There were murmurs from the pews.

"Someone should stop her," said a stout man in a brusque voice.

"Oh, the poor child," whispered a white-haired widow.

"Such a tragic accident," came a hushed sigh.

Some people stared. Others turned away, unable to watch.

Hattie and Nell sat hip-to-hip, their eyebrows cocked in arched bows aimed straight at Virginia.

The front of the church held Matthias's carvings. Her favorite was

one he'd sculpted of St. Mary
Magdalene's ascension. She was
surrounded by angels who were placing
a crown of laurels on her head. Mary
had the sweetest, most innocent smile.
And Virginia knew everything would be
okay.

An excerpt from...

MOTH MEN

written by Christopher Tucker
illustrated by Edward Tucker

I.

In late Spring of '97, an early morning fog rolled off the deep Ohio River blanketing the wide riverbanks of Vandalia County. It shrouded all and left the world to be only what one could see immediately. We drove through the endless grey, my father and I, along Route Two headed out of Kyova Landing. Our destination was Minkawen Marsh.

I sat in the front seat of the family hatchback next to Dad. At nine years old, I believed my father could defeat all-comers because he was an Eagle Scout with a pocket knife. This was the man to be looked up at for me, a short kid who liked video games, books, and spending time with my dad, but especially video games. Books only made the list because we didn't have cable, a budgetary sacrifice due to my father running his own business. Because he was self-employed, time with him wasn't an everyday occurrence which meant when it did happen, that time was a treasure we shared eagerly. Him, by taking me outside in nature. Me, by informing him about video games.

Clutched in my mitts on that morning was a Gameboy with the Pocket Monsters cartridge inserted. That game was my world. I knew playing it in front of a parent would draw inevitable ire, but that morning my father preferred to listen to the radio. Big band swing music from an era I could barely understand. I'm sure Pocket Monsters was equally baffling to him. We each had our thing and this symbiosis between father and son lasted until the radio played a song my father didn't like, so he turned it off. In the quiet that followed, the sounds of my Gameboy bleeped and blooped. The repetitive noise must have worn my father's patience down. He made a strong suggestion in a tone that lacked a question mark.

"Why don't you turn that off? The fog's rolling back, and you can see farther, all the way to the trees." My father said. He wasn't wrong. "It's gonna be dark going home, so you won't be able to see much outside. Don't want to miss it."

For a moment, I considered the fact that my father might be incredibly stupid. Did he truly not know? I held up my Gameboy in response. Playing my game was way better than whatever was out there.

"But the batteries, how long will they last if you keep playing it now?" Dad said. I weighed what I knew about the battery life of a Gameboy versus what secret knowledge my father might possess.

I clicked it off. He won this battle.

Peering out as instructed, I noticed the fog had indeed rolled back a few dozen feet to reveal woods and open fields. Across the way, on the driver's side, the river was visible but I had to look around my father's arms and hands on the steering wheel for a glimpse. There was now much to see on either side of the road. Many buildings in this rural part of Vandalia County were of poor condition with a few appearing on the verge of collapse. They'd been there forever. From the window on my side, I saw houses built far apart with large yards and crop fields butting up against the mountainous hills beyond. Ornaments decorated most lawns and represented the wild palette of the nearby flea market. Besides the common gnome, flamingo, and flags, there were car parts, religious sculptures, dummy deer shot to hell from target practice, and my utmost favorite—old ceramic commodes cleaned up to their alabaster shine. Maybe Dad was right, there was something worth seeing here.

The smile from these delights left my face when we drove past a house with a barbwire fence. Fastened to it were large NO TRESPASSING signs. I asked my father about the people who lived there. They seemed mean. He hummed softly before answering, collecting his thoughts.

"I don't think they're mean. They like open space and being left alone." My father said, "What would you think about living out here? We could walk to the river, go fishing every day if we wanted. It'd be different."

Though his words were absent-minded, they put a fear in me that we might move out here. It didn't feel safe. Sensing my unease, Dad pivoted to a subject he knew was sure to get my attention.

"Have you heard of the Moth Man?" My father asked. "It's a legend around here."

I had not heard of the Moth Man and demanded rectification. Dad obliged.

"A long time ago, before you were born, there was an old Army base near here that had a big accident at the end of World War Two. Some kind of explosion." My father said. "After that, people started seeing weird stuff in the woods and marsh, a creature they called the Moth Man."

My father's tactic was super effective. I had forgotten all about the unfriendly house and the implications of its signs. Eager to know more, I peppered him with questions in search of the full picture.

"I don't know why they call it that." Dad said, "The Moth Man don't have an exact look really. People report seeing all sorts of versions. They're here to warn us from danger, or so the stories say."

Did Dad think that was true?

"I don't know if they're real. The accident was real. It was an explosion. Before it happened, people said they saw the Moth Man. They didn't know it was a warning until it was too late though." My father added, "Don't worry, it's not scary."

My imagination pictured the Moth Man as a huge bug with feathery dark wings and glow-in-the-dark eyes. I had drawn inspiration largely from the monster-filled video game I'd been playing, and possibly other sources.

Once settled on this version of the creature, the rest of the conversation became one-sided as I barraged my father with more questions about the Moth Man that he couldn't possibly know. I can't remember exactly what I asked. When he'd had enough, Dad switched the radio back on. Turning to my window, I searched the parts of the landscape still fog-hidden cosmically certain that the Moth Man lurked beyond the edge of sight.